One named Peter,

one named Paul.

Come back, Peter...

Two Little Dickie Birds
sitting on a wall

Adapted by Russell Punter

Illustrated by Vanessa Port

Two little dickie birds, sitting on a wall.

...come back, Paul.

Two little honey bees, sitting on a daisy.

One named
Mabel,

one named
Maisy.

Buzz away, Mabel!

Buzz away, Maisy!

Come back, Mabel...

...come back, Maisy.

Two little spotted frogs,
sitting on a lily.

One named Bella,

one named Billy.

Hop away, Bella!

Hop away, Billy!

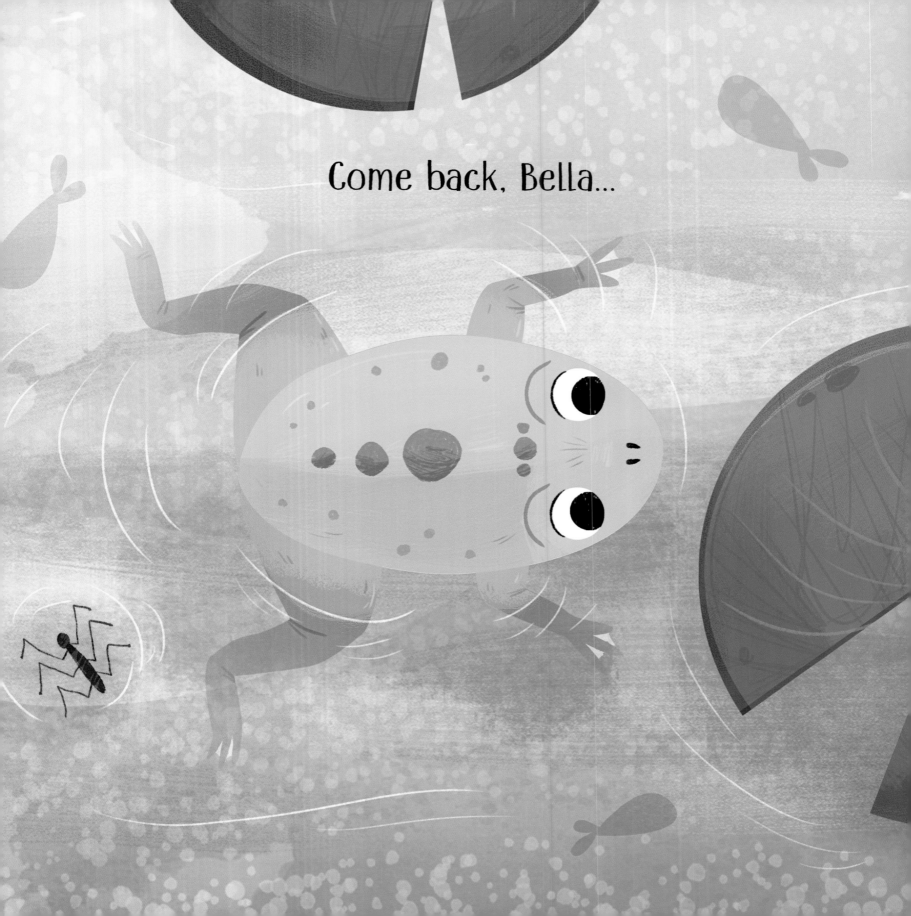

Come back, Bella...

...come back, Billy.

Two little hedgehogs, snuffling by a shed.

One named
Freda,

one named Fred.

Shuffle off,
Freda!

Shuffle off,
Fred!

Come back, Freda...

...come back, Fred.

Two little dickie birds, snuggled in a nest.

They feel sleepy.

Time to rest.

Night night, Peter,

night night, Paul.

Night night
everyone...

Sleep tight all!

Designed by Vickie Robinson
Edited by Lesley Sims